Copyright © 2024 All rights reserved.
No part of this publication may be reproduced, stored in a retrieval system, or transmitted in any form or by any means, electronic, mechanical, photocopying, recording, or otherwise, without prior written permission of the copyright holder, except in the case of brief quotations embodied in critical articles and reviews.
For information regarding permission, e-mail contact@sophieandstephie.com.

This is a work of fiction. Any references to historical events, real people, or real places are used fictitiously. Names, characters, places, and events are products of the author's imagination. Any resemblance to actual persons, living or dead, events, or locales is entirely coincidental.

ISBN:
Paperback 978-1-7363176-4-8
E-book 978-1-959490-28-9

Edited by Chelsea Jackson and Lor Bingham
Cover Design by Praise Saflor

Published by Kids World Press

It's time to get ready for our trip to Hawai'i!

HAWAI'I
Color the map.

KAUA'I

O'AHU

MOLOKA'I

LĀNA'I

MAUI

THE BIG ISLAND

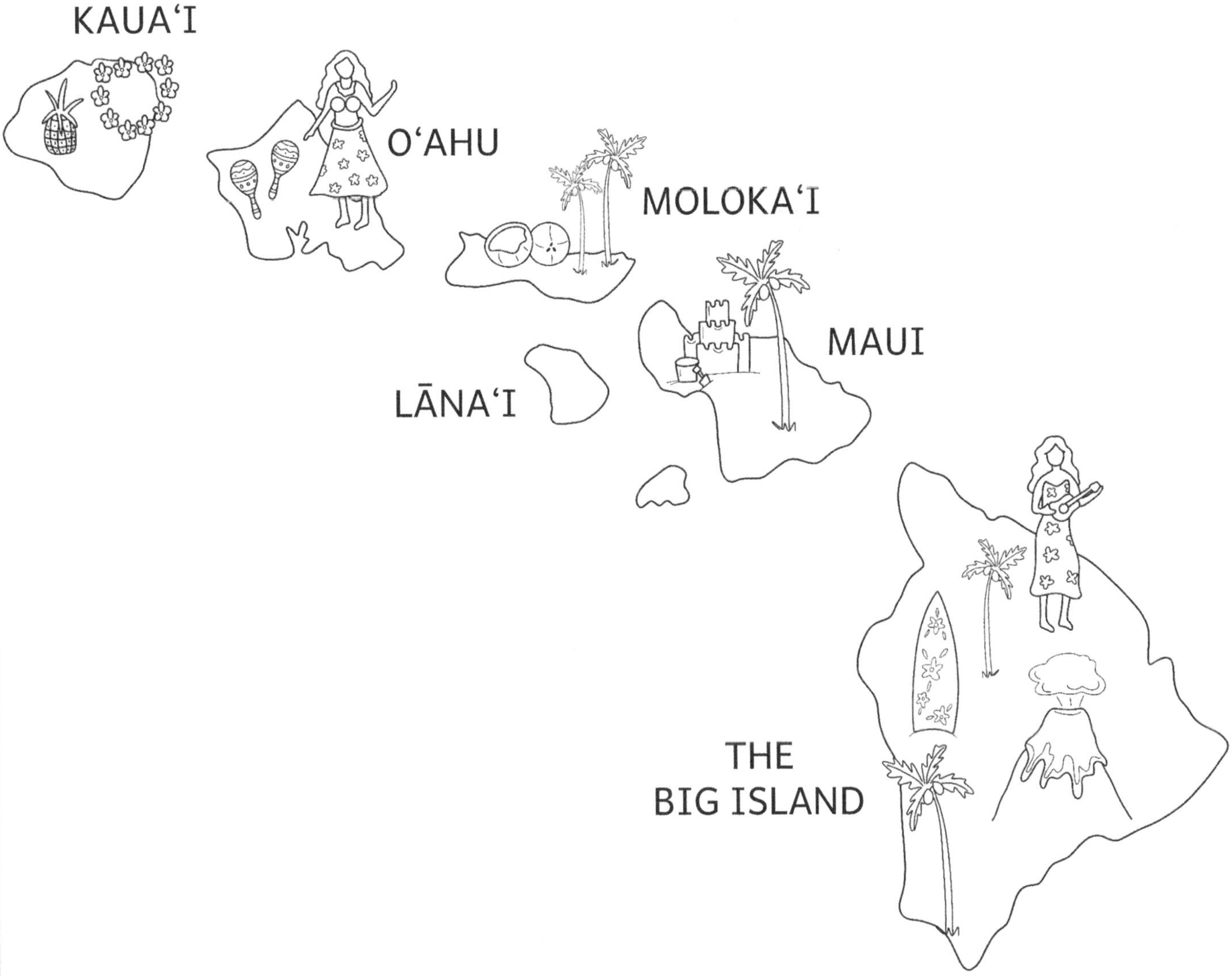

MAZE

Can you help us find Roosevelt?

SPOT THE DIFFERENCES

Spot five (5) differences between the pictures below.

7

WORD SEARCH

```
M A H A L O X L I H O N U E S
G O S Q K E N D Ū ' K F E K Y E
K A T T Q O W F J A L O H A O
F W I D J R L E I O U G H H L
P E C K V G H Y M Z F B O O W
H F T H A W A I ' I A M S W N W
U T I F I P O I I X U C D O T
L H R P P N B L K V T X T L X
A J Q Z Q Ē K C F G X P V U S
I R M A U N A V B X M E U L O
X P Y U I Ē D P G K D D Y U N
```

Find the following words:

LEI   NĒNĒ

HONU   HULA

LŪ'AU   HAWAI'I

ALOHA   MAUNA

MAHALO   HONOLULU

DRAW

Draw three (3) things you would like to do in Hawai'i.

WRITE AN ARTICLE

TRAVEL NEWS

BEST THINGS TO DO IN HAWAIʻI

CROSSWORD PUZZLE

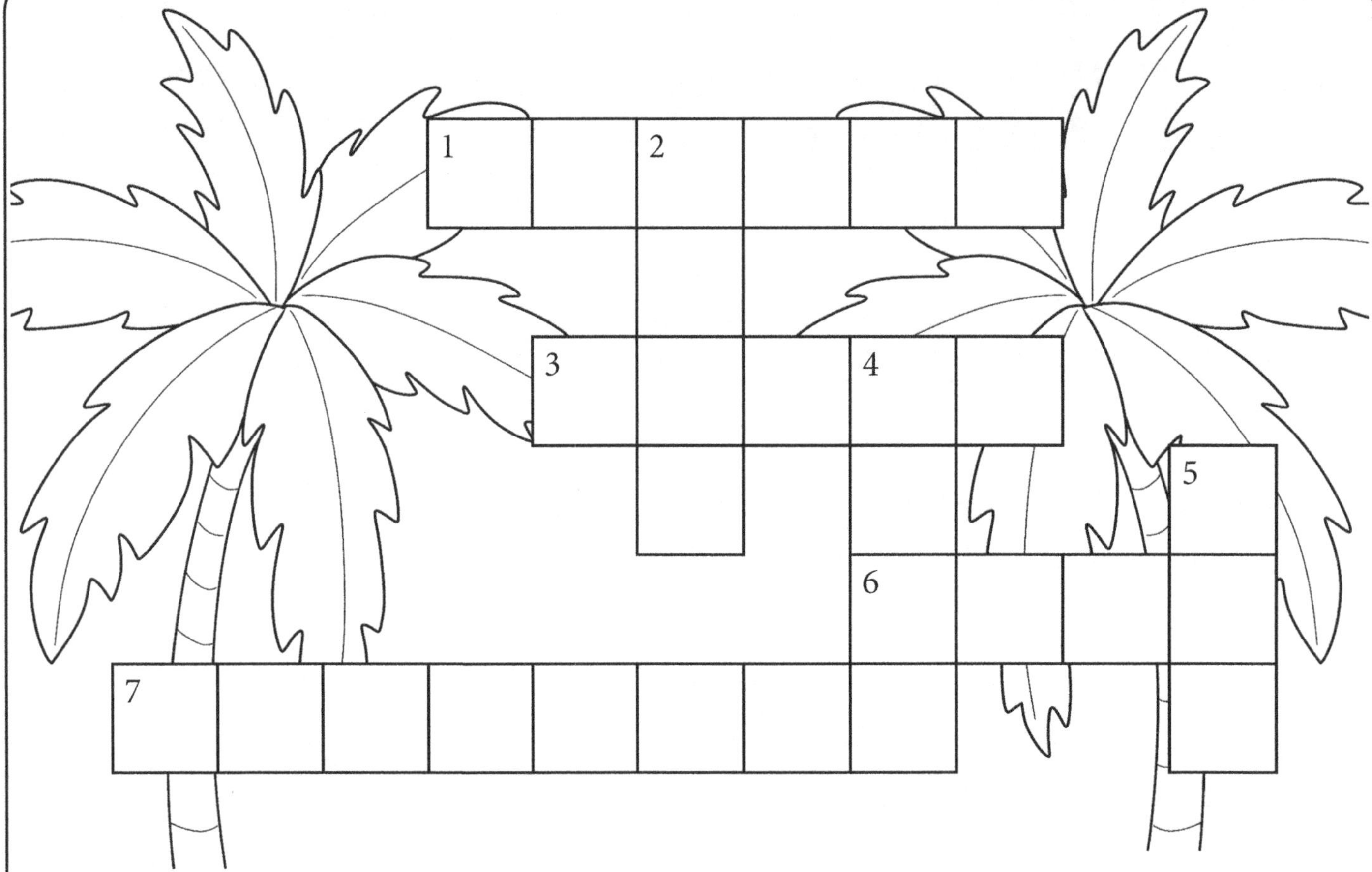

Down:
2. Hawaiian dance
4. "Turtle" in Hawaiian
5. Hawaiian flower necklace

Across:
1. "Thank you" in Hawaiian
3. "Hello" in Hawaiian
6. Hawaiian goose
7. Capital of Hawai'i

WORD BANK

LEI	HONU
HULA	ALOHA
NĒNĒ	MAHALO
HONOLULU	

SQUARE UP

Cut out the images at the bottom of the page. Fill in the remaining empty boxes with the pictures of each of the four images. Each image can only appear once in each row and once in each column.

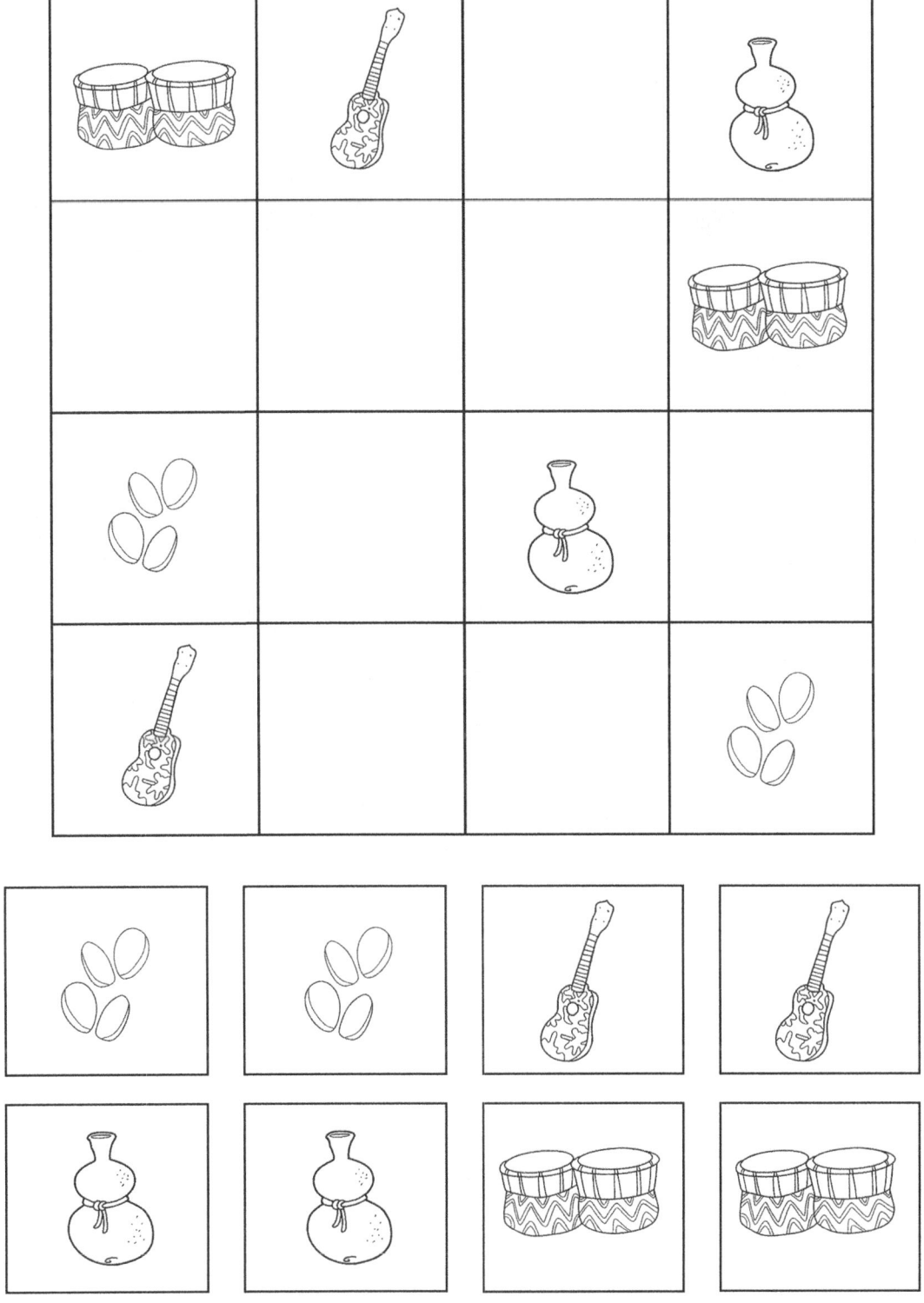

CONNECT THE DOTS

DRAW

Using the grid, copy the picture of the nēnē—the Hawaiian goose.

CRACK THE CODE

In the puzzle below, each picture represents a different letter of the alphabet. Figure out the code and use it to reveal the word.

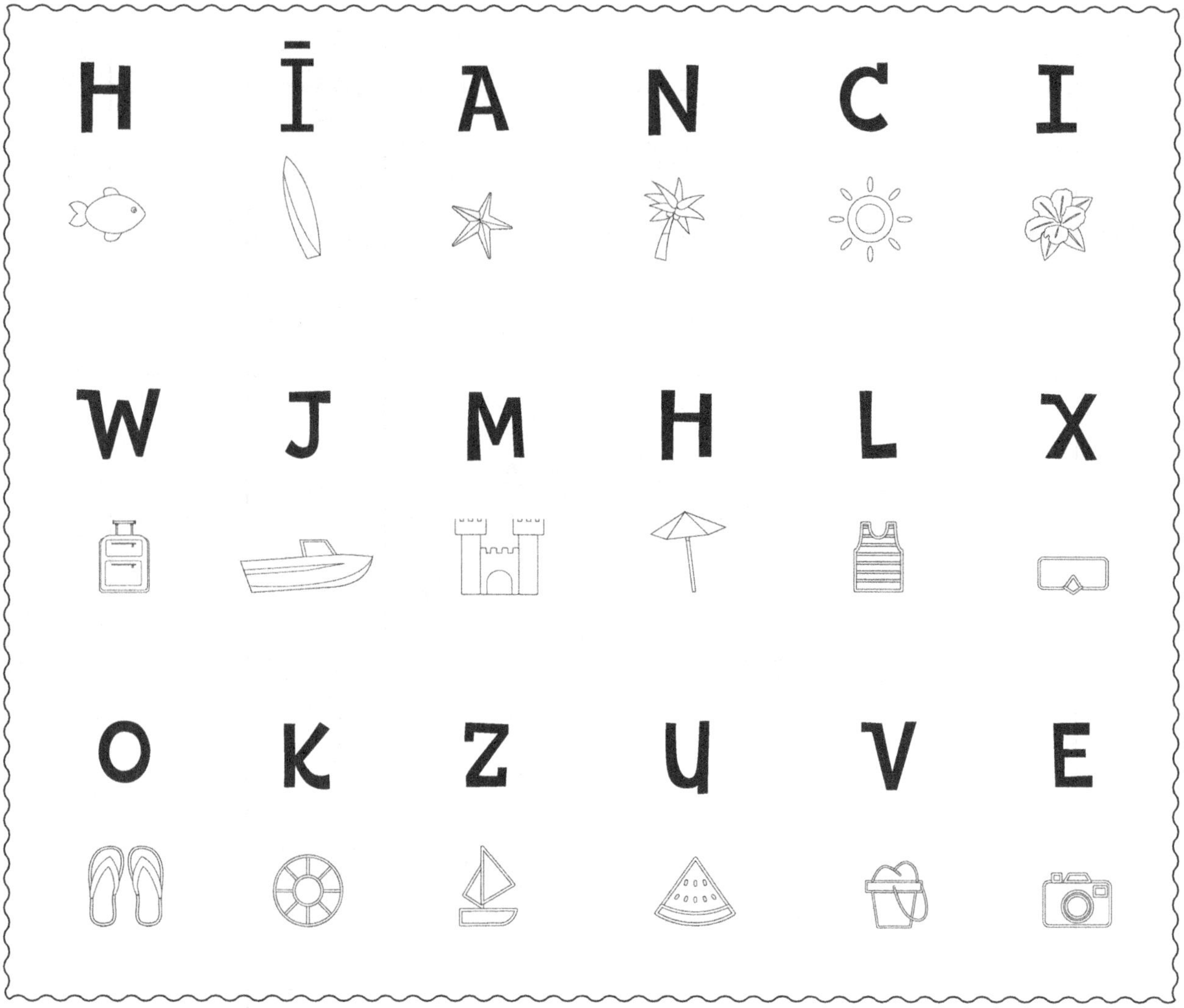

H	Ī	A	N	C	I
🐟	🏄	⭐	🌴	☀️	🌺

W	J	M	H	L	X
🧳	🚤	🏰	⛱️	👕	🥽

O	K	Z	U	V	E
👡	🛟	⛵	🍉	🪣	📷

Mystery Word Reveal!

WHICH PICTURE IS DIFFERENT?

Color the picture that is different than the rest.

1

2

3

4

5

6

7

8

9

TAKE US ON THE TRIP!

Connect the following items to the Travel Sisters.

CRACK THE CODE

In the puzzle below, each picture represents a different letter of the alphabet. Figure out the code and use it to reveal the words.

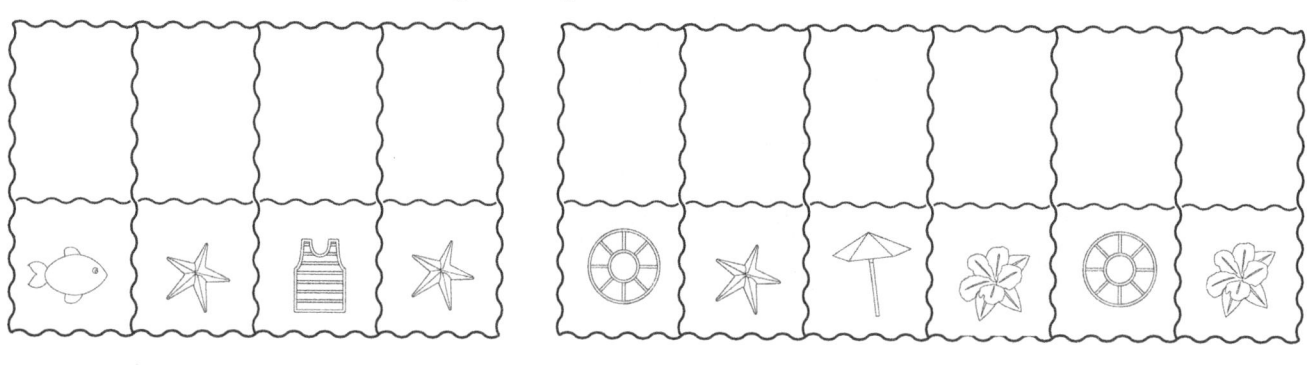

Mystery Words Reveal!

COUNT THE LEIS

How many leis can you find in the image below?

LEIS:

WHICH PICTURE IS DIFFERENT?

Color the picture that is different than the rest.

1

2

3

4

5

6

7

8

9

DRAWING

Using the grid, copy the picture of the volcano.

TRACE AND COLOR

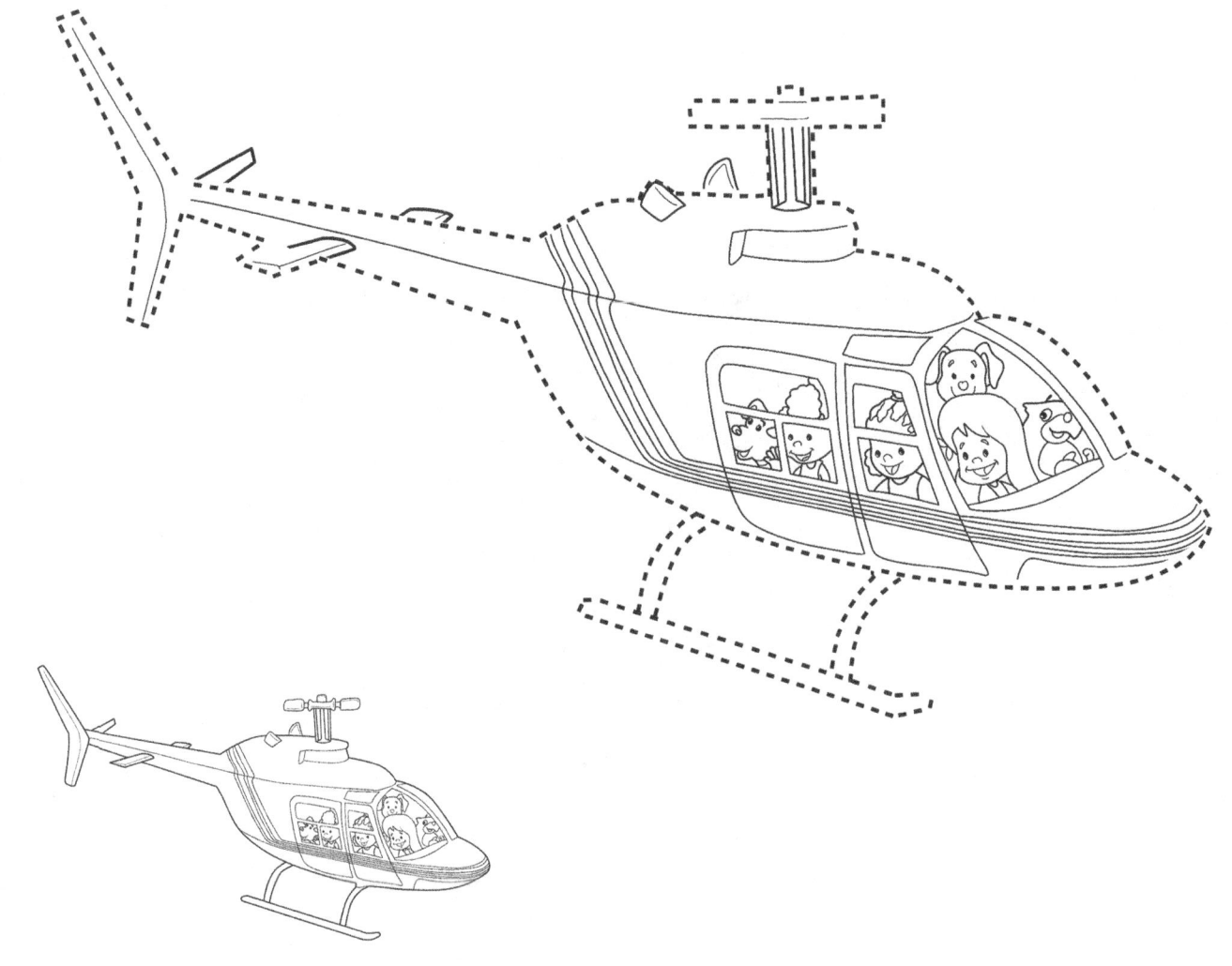

FIND THE MISSING PIECE

Roosevelt's lei is missing! Cut out the lei and paste it on his head.

ADD THE PICTURES

Write the answers in the empty boxes.

 +  =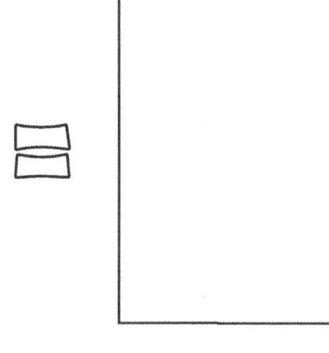

 +  =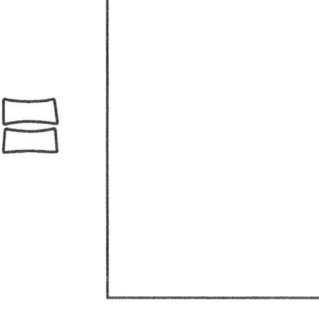

29

MATCH THE SHADOW

Draw a line from each image to its shadow.

DRAW AND COLOR

Using the grid, copy the picture of the honu—turtle and color it.

SUBTRACT THE PICTURES

Write the answers in the empty boxes.

 − 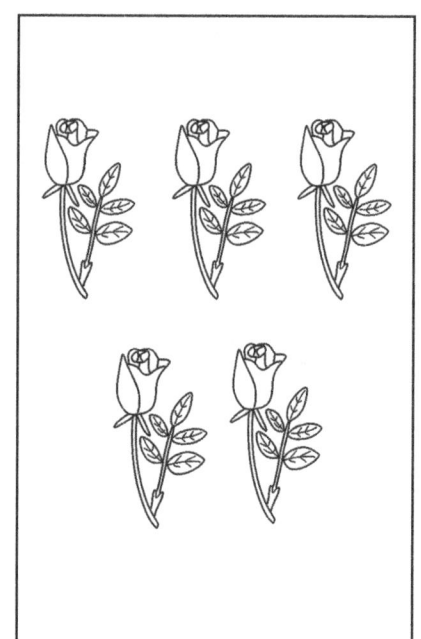 =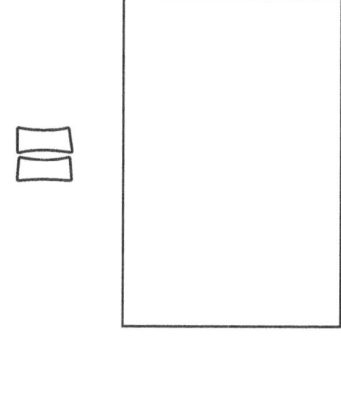

 −  =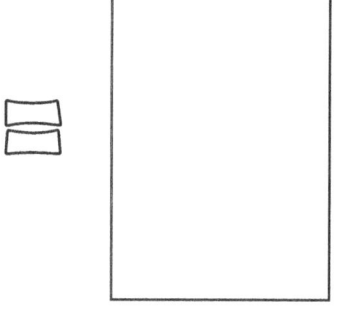

FINISH THE DRAWING

Complete the drawing by finishing the other half of the grid.

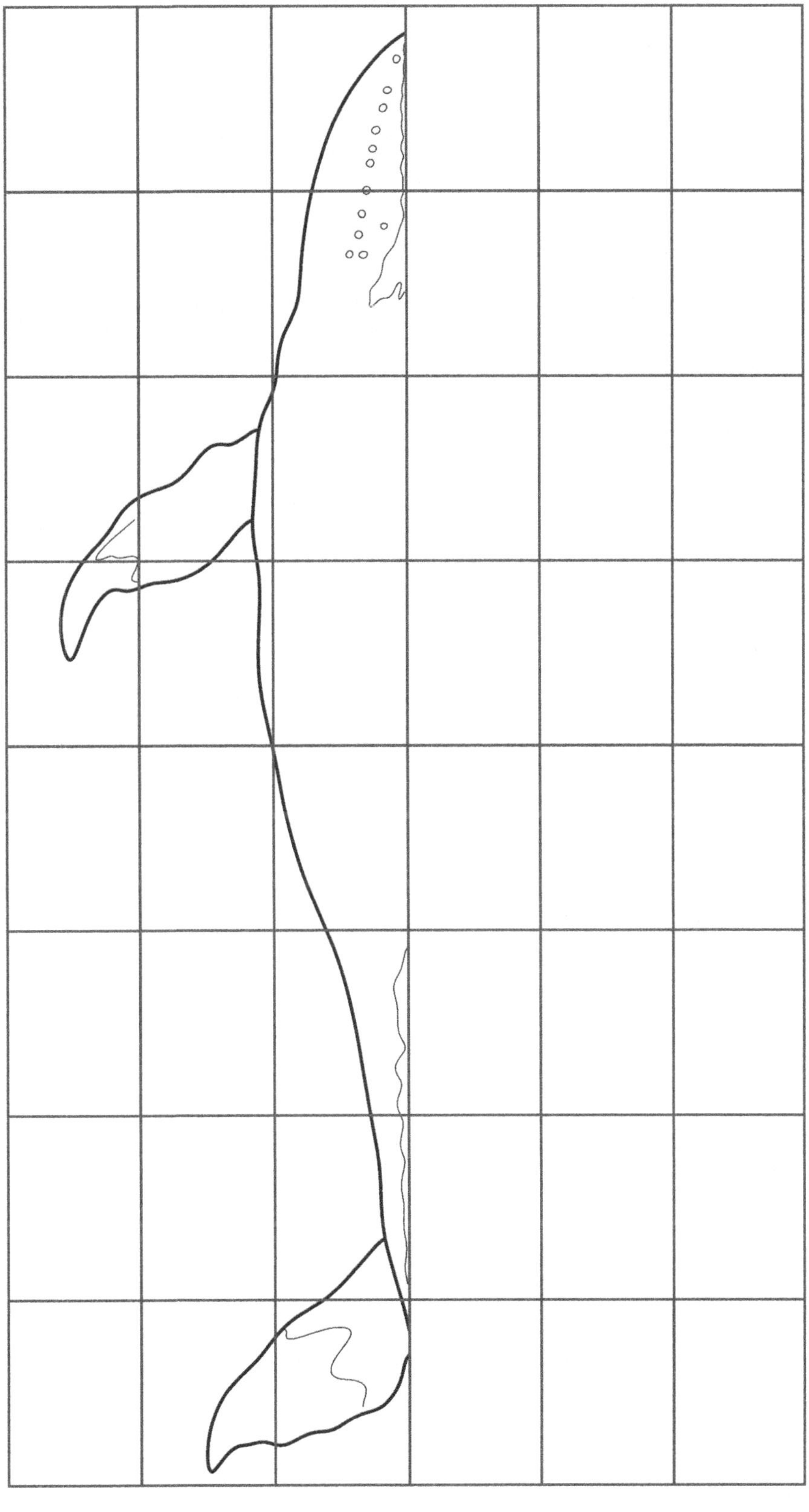

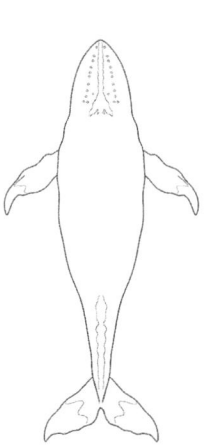

37

SUBTRACT THE PICTURES

Write the answers in the empty boxes.

 −  =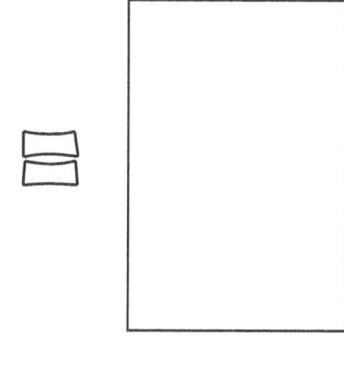

 −  =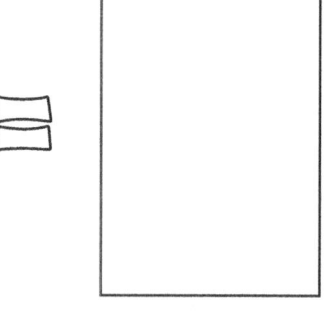

MAZE

Can you help us find Stephie and Roosevelt?

39

SQUARE UP

Cut out the images at the bottom of the page. Fill in the remaining empty boxes with the pictures of each of the four images. Each image can only appear once in each row and once in each column.

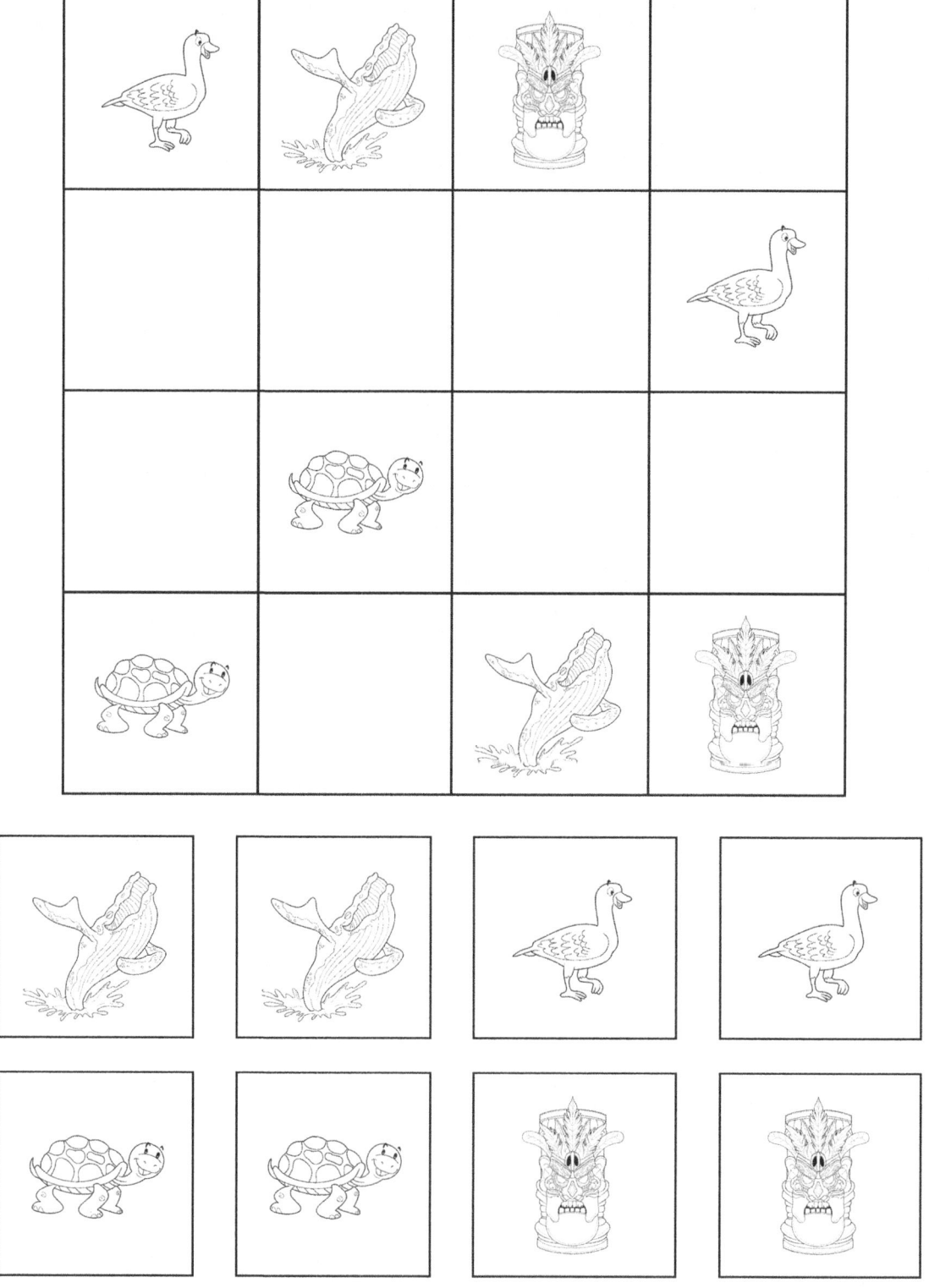

WHICH PICTURE IS DIFFERENT?

Color the picture that is different than the rest.

1

2

3

4

5

6

7

8

9

SPOT THE DIFFERENCES

Spot five (5) differences between the pictures below.

READ AROUND

Read around to reveal the mystery word!

Start at the letter "A" below Squawking. Write letter "A" in the first letter bubble below. Skip four letters to the right (clockwise). Write that letter in the mystery word's second letter bubble. Now write every fifth letter in the letter bubbles until you return to Squawking and discover the mystery word!

A L O H A

44

CONNECT THE DOTS

TIC-TAC-TOE

Color the images below. Cut them out and play Tic-Tac-Toe.

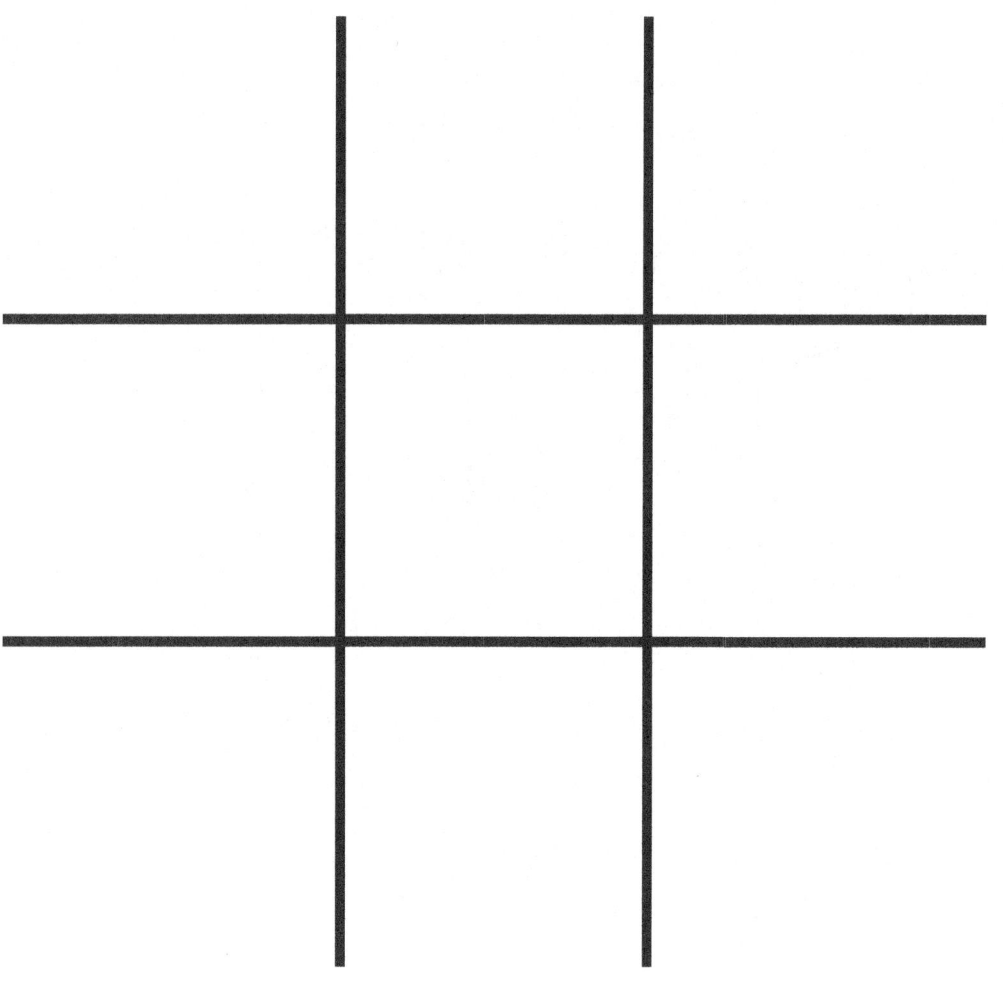

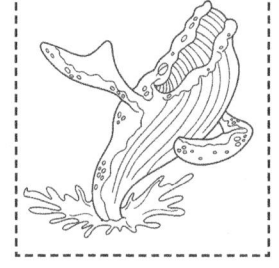    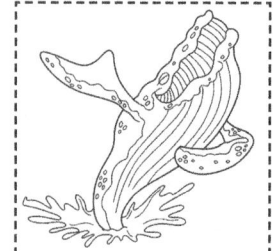

WHICH PICTURE IS DIFFERENT?

Color the picture that is different than the rest.

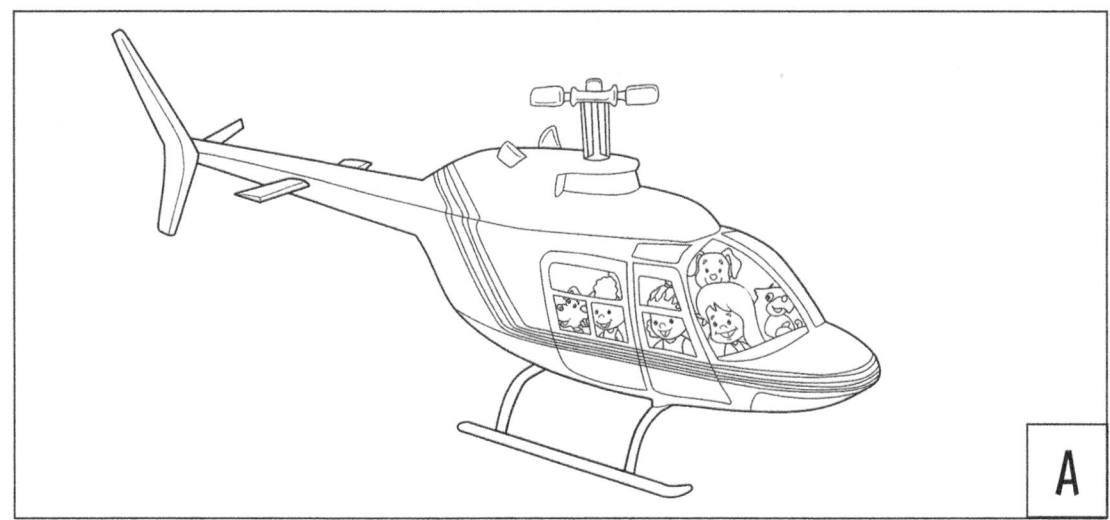

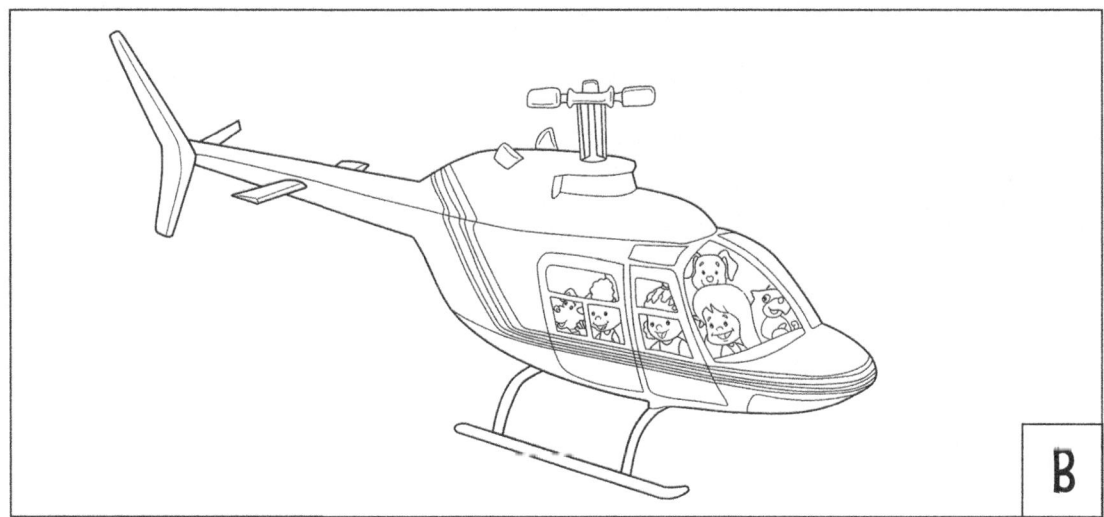

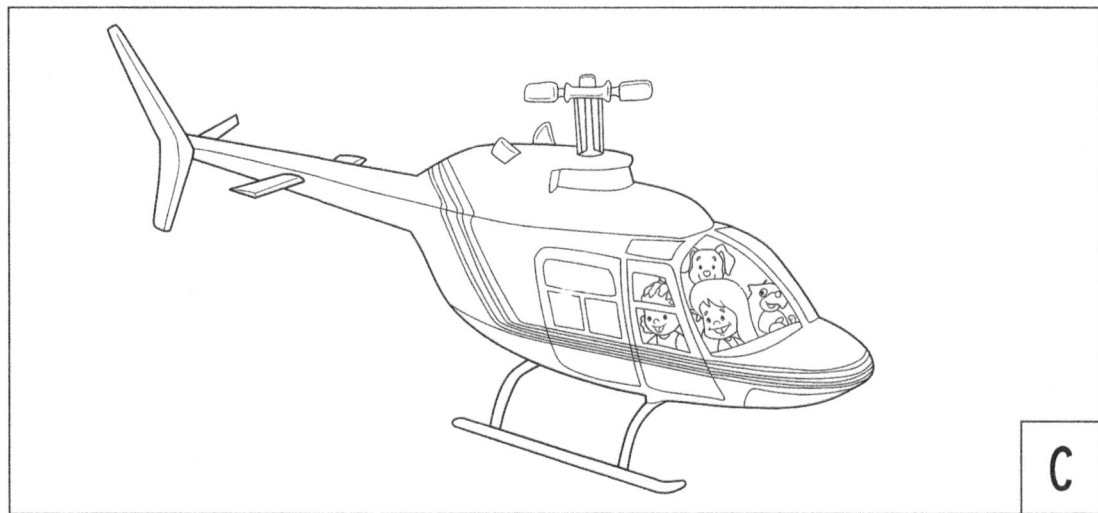

FINISH THE DRAWING

Complete the drawing by finishing the other half of the grid.

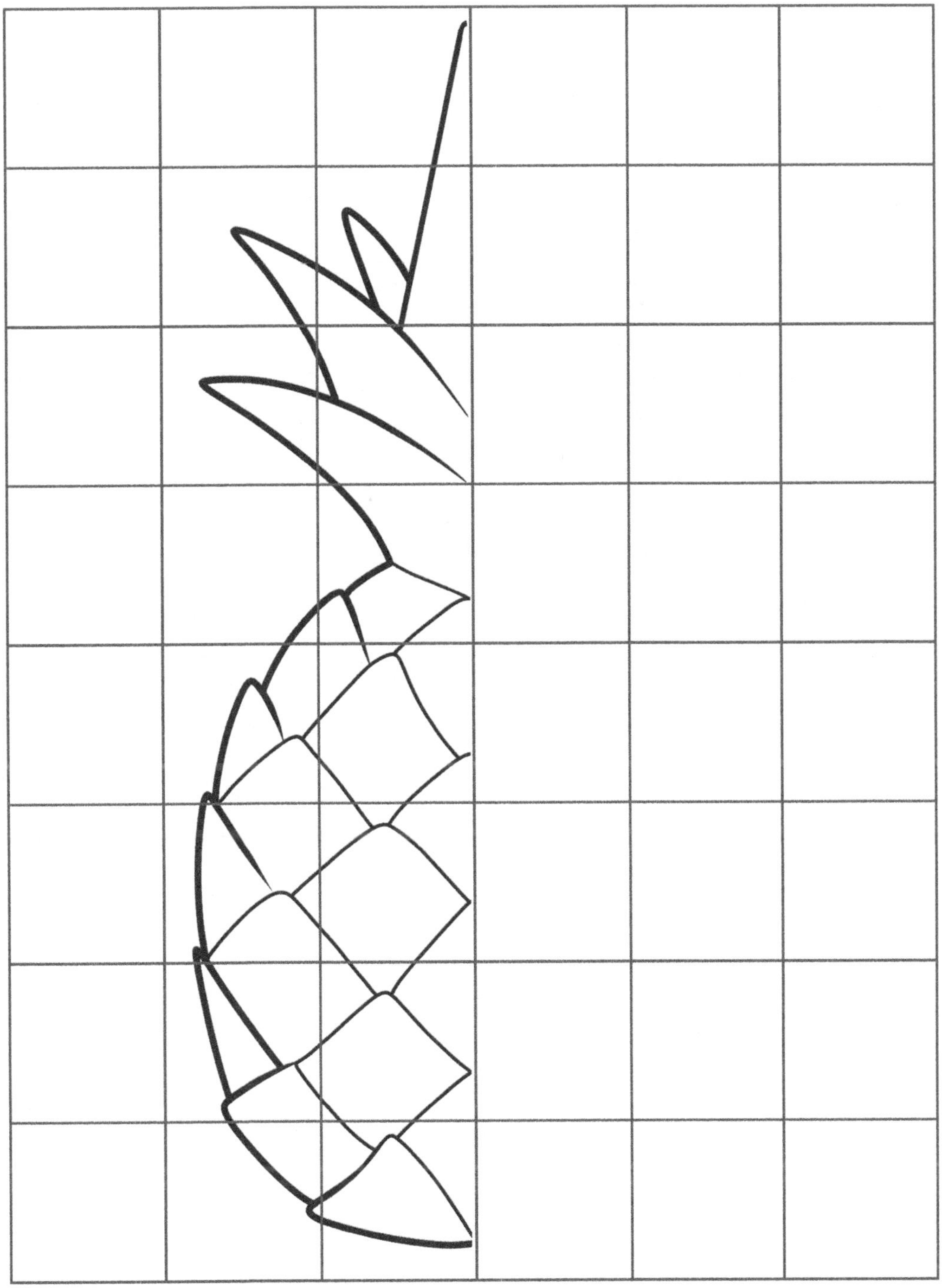

COMPLETE THE MISSING PARTS

Spot three (3) differences and complete the picture.

50

WHICH PICTURE IS DIFFERENT?

Color the picture that is different than the rest.

A

B

C

D

ADD THE PICTURES

Write the answers in the empty boxes.

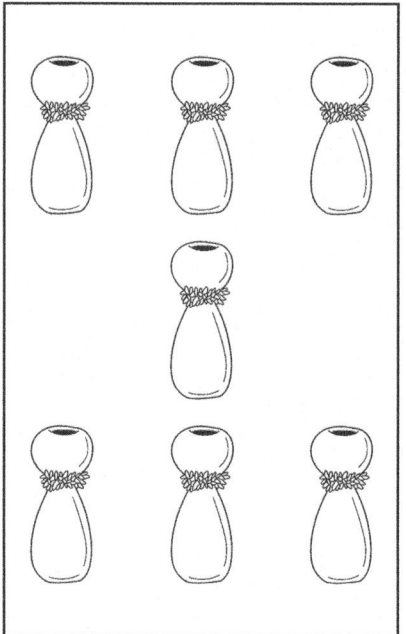 + 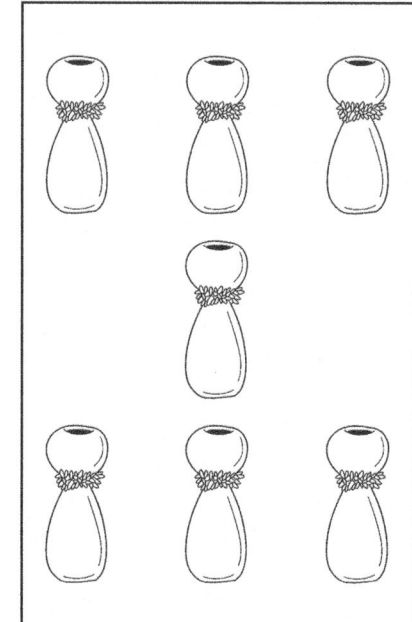 =

 +  =

52

DECORATE A MASK

MATCHING GAME

Match the word with the correct flower.

KAUNA'OA

MOKIHANA

LOKELANI

LEHUA

'ILIMA

UNSCRAMBLE THE WORDS

'UUKLLEE

_ _ _ _ _ _ _

HNOOLULU

_ _ _ _ _ _ _ _

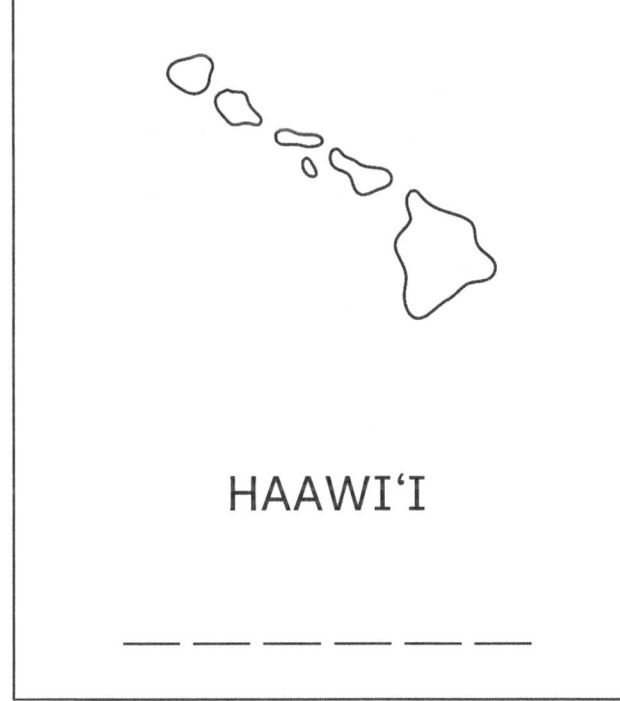

HAAWI'I

_ _ _ _ _ _ _

UHLA

_ _ _ _

PUT THE STORY IN ORDER

Put the story in order by writing 1, 2, 3, or 4 in the circle on each image.

WHAT HAPPENS NEXT?

What do you think happens after the Travel Sisters win the Floral Parade?

Draw a picture that shows what happens.

ANSWER KEYS

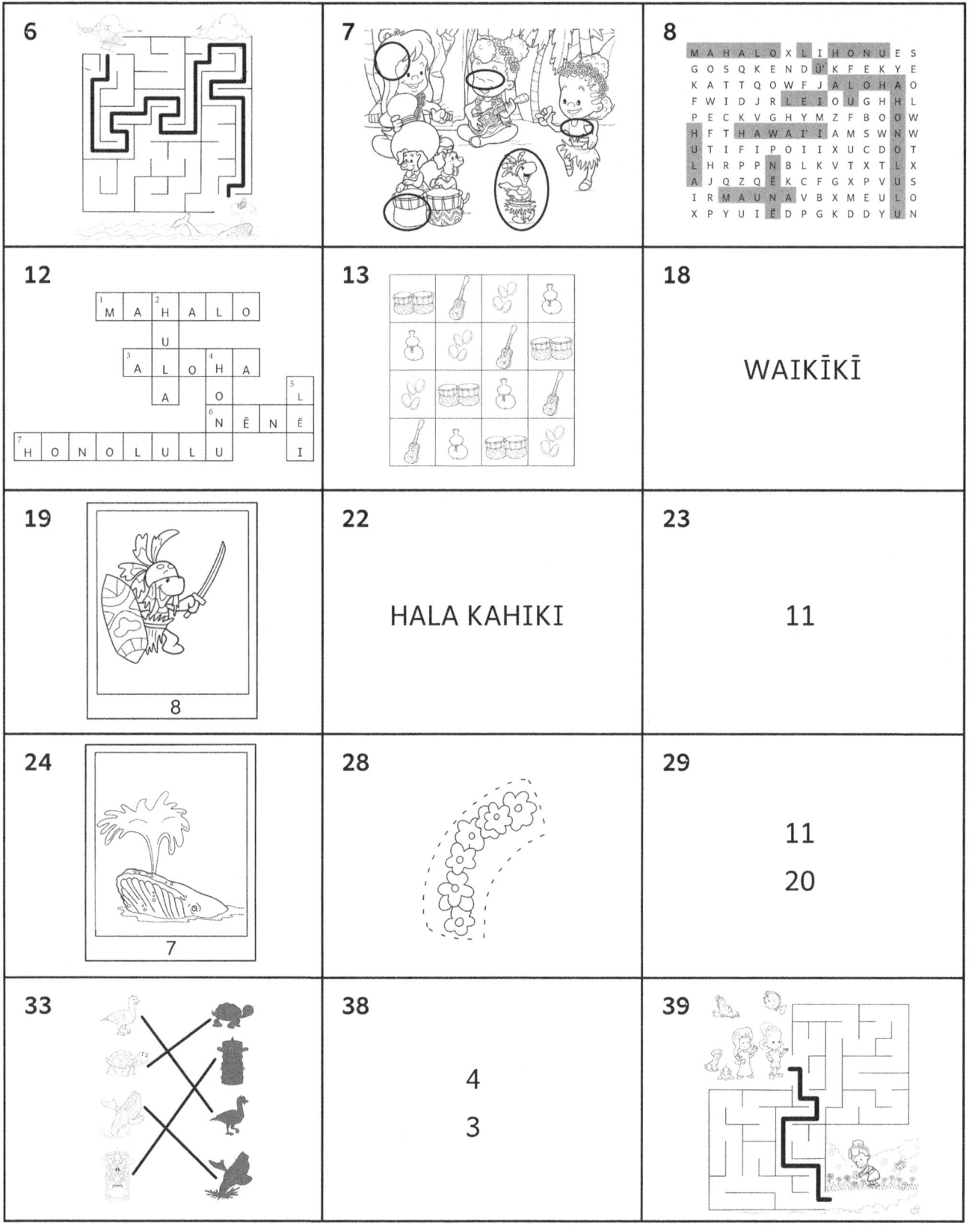

ANSWER KEYS

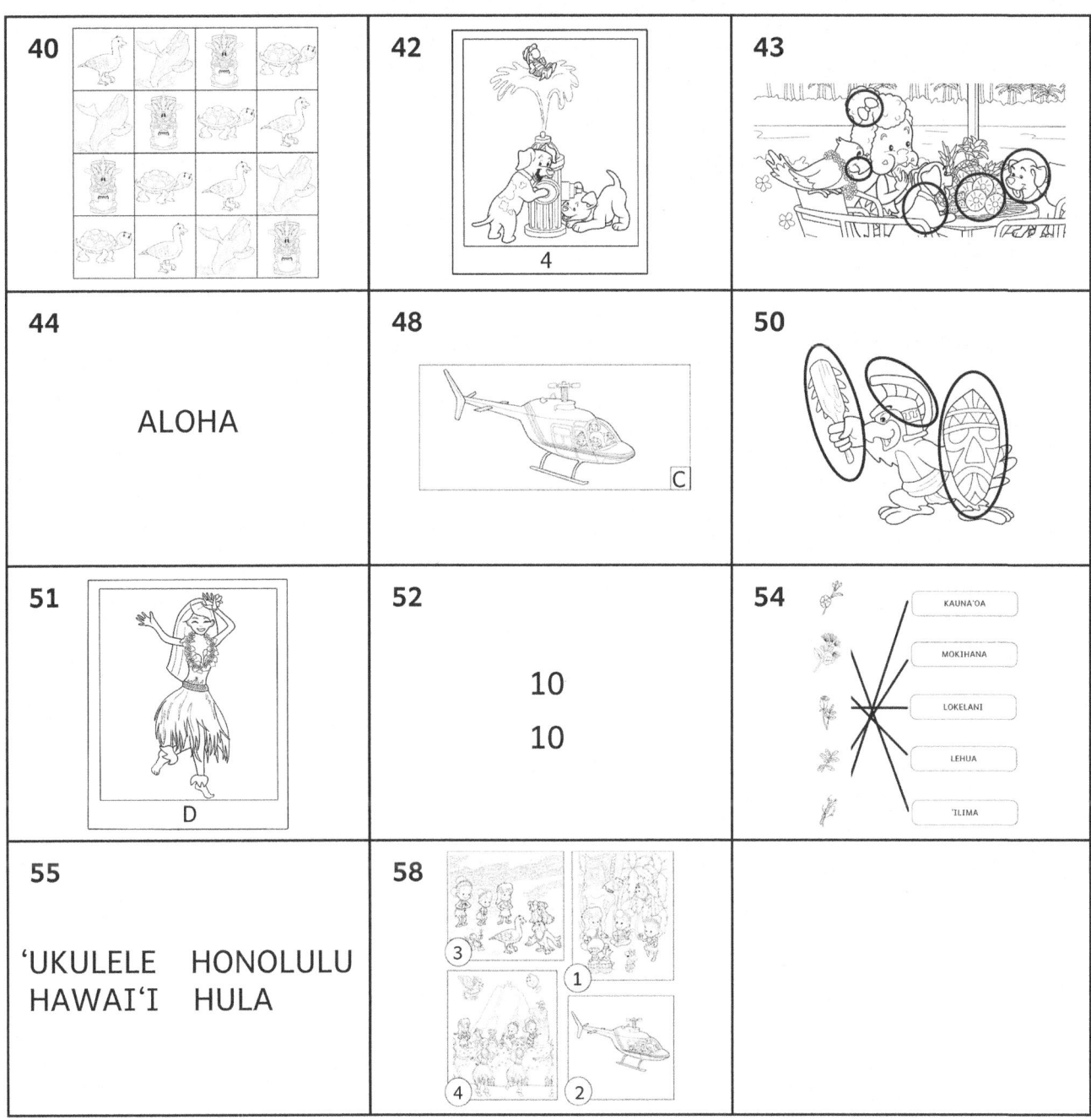

THANK YOU for your purchase!

If you loved this activity book, please leave a **REVIEW**.
For additional resources and free downloads,
visit **www.sophieandstephie.com** or scan the **QR code** below.

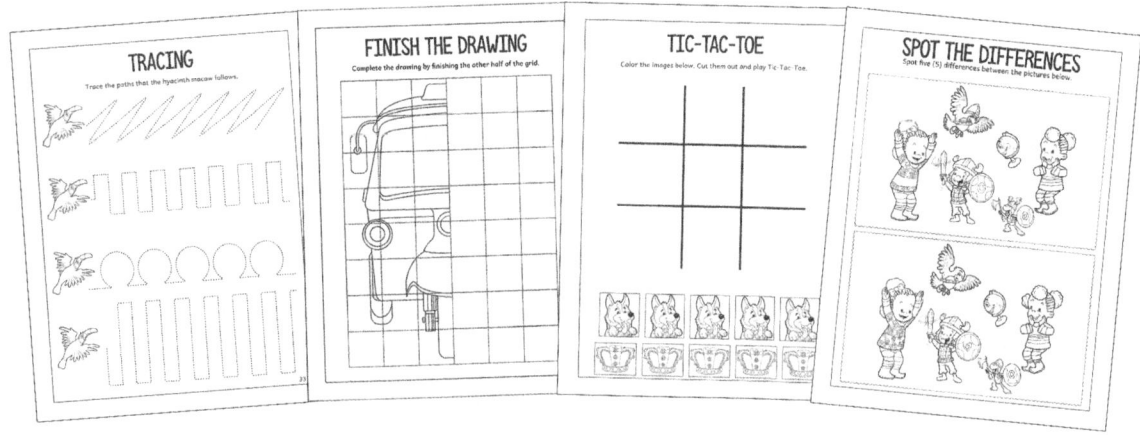

Ekaterina Otiko
& The Travel Sisters Team

Made in the USA
Las Vegas, NV
07 November 2024

11298752R00037